The Way of Ecben

*A
Comedietta
Involving a
Gentleman*

BOOKS BY MR. CABELL

BIOGRAPHY:

Beyond Life
Figures of Earth
The Silver Stallion
Domnei
The Music from Behind the Moon
Chivalry
Jurgen
The Line of Love
The High Place
Gallantry
Something About Eve
The Certain Hour
The Cords of Vanity
From the Hidden Way
The Jewel Merchants
The Rivet in Grandfather's Neck
The Eagle's Shadow
The Cream of the Jest
The Lineage of Lichfield
Straws and Prayer-Books
Townsend of Lichfield

∽

James Branch Cabell (*by Carl Van Doren*)
James Branch Cabell (*by H. L. Mencken*)
The Art of James Branch Cabell (*by Hugh Walpole*)
Cabellian Harmonics (*by Warren A. McNeill*)
A Round-Table in Poictesme (*Edited by Don Bregenzer and Samuel Loveman*)
Jurgen and the Censor (*Edited by Barrett H. Clark*)
Bibliography of James Branch Cabell (*by Guy Holt*)

The Way of Ecben

A Comedietta Involving a Gentleman

by

James Branch Cabell

Decorations by Frank C. Papé

*"I go the way of all the earth: be thou strong therefore,
and show thyself a man; and keep the charge of thy god,
to walk in his way and preserve his testimonies."*

New York

Robert M. McBride & Company

1929

Printed in the United States of America
By the Plimpton Press, Norwood, Massachusetts

For

ROBERT M. MCBRIDE
this brief and somewhat tragic tale, to
commemorate our long and rather
comical association

Contents

Contents

Synopsis

Songs from *Antan* behind the moon delay
What line of hidden white-robed life, beyond
Old Jurgen's judging, in that Eve's high wand
Taboos all music, if but as eagles may?
Figures of love, these sonnets' souls repay
Proud earth with gallantry; and rivet Eve
With something about merchants — to reprieve
With silver, and with jewels, Ecben's way.

Grandfathers *wake, with prayer-books and cords,*
The cream of chivalry; and stallions rightly
Deride the shadow of a lineage, lords
To domnei's straws of vanity; while nightly
The jest of Lichfield moves toward place and power
The certain town's end of a neck's last hour.

Words for the Intending Reader

Words for the Intending Reader

NOBODY will think, I hope, that I pretend to have invented this story. Those who are familiar with the earlier works of Felix Kennaston will of course recognize that one encounters hereinafter the Norrovian legend upon which is based *The King's Quest*. There has never been, though, so far as I am aware, any prose version made in English; and in taking over this story from Garnier's anthology, Kennaston necessarily introduced many and frequent changes prompted by the demands of Spenserian verse.

Moreover, Kennaston—with, as I think, unwisdom—has toiled to prettify the tale throughout, and to point, a bit laboriously, an apologue which in the story's original form simply does not exist. I may at least assert that in *The Way of Ecben* (which "teaches" nothing whatever) I have clung rigorously to the queer legend's restrained, and quite unfigurative, first shaping.

—This, too, under some duress. The tale is so brief that in recording it the temptation was ever present to pad here and there, and to enlarge upon one or another detail, with the wholly pardonable design of rewarding each possible purchaser with the average amount of reading-matter to be found in the average novel of commerce. . . . But in the outcome I have

Words for the Intending Reader

resisted that ever-present temptation. For Garnier knew his business; the thing as it stands is properly proportioned: and symmetry is, after all, one of the seven great auctorial virtues.

Richmond-in-Virginia
April, 1929

PART ONE

OF ALFGAR IN HIS KINGDOM

*" What the King Wishes,
the Law Wills."*

CHAPTER ONE

The Warring for Ettaine

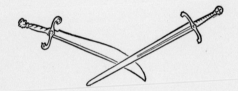

CHAPTER ONE

The Warring for Ettaine

IT IS an old tale which tells of the fighting between Alfgar, the King of Ecben, and Ulf, the King of Rorn. Their enmity took hold of them because they both desired that daughter of Thordis who was called Ettaine.

Two kings desired her because of all the women of this world Ettaine was the most beautiful. It was the blue of her eyes, that had the brightness of the spring sky when there is no cloud anywhere between heaven and the heads of men, which caused the armies of Rorn and of Ecben to meet like thunder clouds. Blood was spilled everywhere because of that red which was in the lips of Ettaine. The golden flaming of her hair burned down into black cinders the towns of Rorn and of Ecben.

Ulf's fort at Meivod, it is true, withstood all besiegers: but Druim fell, then Tarba. Achren also was taken: its fields were plowed up and planted with salt. Then Ulf captured Sorram, through undermining its walls. But Alfgar took Garian by storm, and he burned this city like- wise, after carrying from it a quantity of cross- bows and tents and two wagon loads of silver.

There was thus no quietness anywhere in that part of the world, because of the comeliness of Ettaine. For two kings desired her: and her color and her shaping thus became a lofty moral issue, with a rich flowering of tumult and of increased taxes, and of corruption and of swift death every- where, and of many very fine patriotic orations.

Then, in the fourth year of the fighting, the unexampled heroism and the superb ideals of the men of Ecben, which one half of these ora- tions had talked about, were handsomely re- warded by the deafness of Cormac. This Cormac of the Twin Hills led a third of the armies of Rorn. He was paid the price of his deafness: for three maidens without any blemish in their bod- ies, and for four bags of blue turquoises, and for the silver which King Alfgar had captured at Garian, this Cormac became deaf to the other half of these orations, now that he betrayed the unexampled heroism and the superb ideals of the men of Rorn.

There was never a more gallant butchering than the patriots of Ecben then gave to the trapped patriots of Rorn under the elm-trees of the ravine at Strathgor. King Ulf alone was spared out of that ruined army where every other fighting-man lay in two halves, like the orations which had delighted them.

So was it that the victory fell to Alfgar. None now withstood him. All that his heart desired he had, and he furthermore had all the forests and the cities and the sleek pastures of Rorn. Ulf, who was not any longer a king, prayed to his gods from out of a well guarded dungeon. And everywhere in Ecben, from green Pen Loegyr to the gaunt hills of Tagd, the barons and their attendants rode toward the King's house in Sorram, and all made ready for the marriage feast of Alfgar the high king and Ettaine the most fair of the women of this world.

CHAPTER TWO

Of Their Love-talk

CHAPTER TWO

Of Their Love-talk

A T THE King's house in Sorram was a hedged garden, with flagstones in the middle of it, about a little fountain: and there King Alfgar and Ettaine would sit and talk in the clear April weather.

" Ettaine of the blue eyes," King Alfgar used to say, " it is not right that your two eyes should be my mirrors. In each of them I find myself. A tiny image of me is set up in their brightness."

" Delight of both my eyes," Ettaine would reply to him, " in my heart also is that image set up."

King Alfgar said: " Ettaine of the red lips, it is not right that your lips should be making for me any music so dear. Some god will be peering out of heaven at my happiness, and a jealousy of me will be troubling that lonely god who has not any such fine music in his heaven."

" For no god and for no heaven whatever," the fair girl answered, " would I be leaving the Alfgar that has the pre-eminent name and is the darling of the women of Ecben. For in his strong arms is my only heaven."

Then Alfgar said: " Ettaine of the bright hair, it is not right that at to-morrow's noon an archbishop will be putting the crown of a queen of Ecben upon your shining head. Ecben is but a little land: and if the brightness of the crowns of Rome and of Byzantium, and of every other kingdom which retains a famousness, had all been shaped into one crown for my Ettaine to be wearing, the brightness of this hair would shame it."

Ettaine answered him, " It is not the crown which is dear to me, O heart of all my happiness, but the king alone."

" Why, but," said Alfgar, " two kings have loved Ettaine."

Whereupon the fond and radiant daughter of Thordis Bent-Neck laughed contentedly, and replied: " Yet to my judgment and to my desires no person is kingly except Alfgar. And, as for that Ulf—!" A shrug rounded off her exact opinion.

Such was the sort of nonsense which these youthful lovers talked upon the eve of their marriage feast, as they sat together in the hedged garden at Sorram, where the pale new grass grew raggedly between the brown flagstones, and the silver jetting of the little fountain wavered everywhither under the irresolute, frail winds of April. And around and above these lovers who were young the young leaves whispered in their merry prophesying of more than a century of summers might by any chance fulfil.

CHAPTER THREE

A Dream Smites Him

CHAPTER THREE

A Dream Smites Him

NOW it was in the night season of his marriage eve that a dream came upon King Alfgar. Through his dreaming a music went wandering. It was a far-off music not very clearly heard, and a music which, he knew, was not of this world. But that there was a sorcery in this bitter music he knew also, for it held him motionless.

The champion that had slain many warriors lay upon his couch, beneath a coverlet of lamb's wool dyed with blue stripings, as still as a slain warrior. Upon him who had all his desires came doubtfulness and discontent. He desired that which this music desired, and which this music quested after, skirlingly, and could not find in any quarter of earth. For it was to the sound of this music, as Alfgar knew, with a troubled heart, that

Horvendile and his Ettarre passed down the years together, and led men out of the set ways of life.

So now a woman came to Alfgar where the King lay upon his couch beneath the coverlet of lamb's wool, and with this woman came a red-haired boy. The woman smiled. The boy smiled also, but his face became white and drawn when he had laid the hand of this woman upon the hand of Alfgar, and when the woman bent downward so that her face was near to Alfgar's face.

She spoke then, putting her command upon Alfgar in the while that he saw her face and the bright glitter of her eyes and the slow moving of her lips. It was in this way that Ettarre the witch-woman, whom a poet fetched out of the gray Waste Beyond the Moon, to live upon our earth in many bodies, now put a memory and a desire and a summoning upon King Alfgar in the hour of his triumph.

Moreover Alfgar now heard, very faintly, and as though from a far distance, a noise of grieving little voices which wailed confusedly. And that remote thin wailing said, —

" All hail, Ettarre! "

A Dream Smites

Then one small voice was saying, " Because of you, we could be contented with no woman." And yet another voice was saying, " Because of you, we got no pleasure from any melody that is of this world." And still a third voice said, " Because of you, we fared among mankind as exiles."

Thereafter all these faint thin voices cried together, " All hail, Ettarre, who took from us contentment, and who led us out of the set ways of life! "

So was it that this dreaming ended. King Alfgar awoke alone in the first light of dawn, and knew that his doom was upon him.

CHAPTER FOUR

The Sending of the Swallow

CHAPTER FOUR

The Sending of the Swallow

NOWHERE in that part of the world was there any king more powerful than Alfgar. Young Alfgar sat upon his throne builded of apple-wood with rivets of copper, and his barons stood about him. Upon his fair high head he wore the holy crown of Ecben, the gift of Ecben's one god: the kingship over all Ecben was his who wore that crown. Gold rings hung in the ears of Alfgar; about the neck of Alfgar were five rings of gold, and over the broad shoulders of Alfgar was a purple robe edged with two strips of vair.

He bade them summon from the women's pleasant galleries Ettaine, the daughter of Thordis Bent-Neck, so that Ettaine might be crowned as Queen over Ecben. He bade them fetch from the dark prison that Ulf who was no longer a king.

Alfgar considered well these two who stood before him. Behind Ettaine were her brdesmaids. These maids were sweetly smiling tall girls, with yellow curling hair and clear blue eyes: each one of these four maids had over her white body a robe of green silk with a gold star upon the tip of each of her young breasts. But behind Ulf two of the masked men in red who had fetched him hither were laying out the implements of their profession, and the other two masked men were quietly kindling a serviceable fire.

The barons of Ecben deferentially suggested such tortures as each baron, during the course of his military or juridical career, had found to be the most prolonged and entertaining to watch. But the archbishop of Ecben took no part in these secular matters: instead, he gallantly fetched a chair of carved yew-wood, and he placed in it a purple cushion sewed with gold threads, so that Ettaine might observe the administration of justice in complete comfort.

Then, while all waited on the will of Alfgar, a swallow darted toward Ulf, and plucked from his defiant dark head a hair, and the bird flew away with this hair dangling from its broad short bill. At that, the barons of Ecben cried out joyously. All were familiar with the Sending of the Swallow: it was a Sending well known to fame and to many honorable legends; for it was in this way that the gods of Rorn were accustomed to put ruin and downfall upon their cousins, the kings of Rorn. So every baron now rejoiced to observe their morning's work thus freely endorsed in advance with the approval of Heaven, now that Ulf's gods forsook him. King Alfgar alone of that merry company kept silence.

Then Alfgar said: "This is the Swallow of Kogi. This is a Sending of the three gods of Rorn. In what forgotten hour did these three take their rule over Ecben?"

"Nevertheless, sire," remarked the archbishop, in a slight flurry, "it is well, and it is much wiser too, to preserve with the gods of every country our diplomatic relations."

But Alfgar answered: "What the king wishes, the law wills. And we of Ecben serve only one god, and one king, and one lady in domnei."

Alfgar descended the red steps of his throne.

He unclasped his robe of purple edged with a king's double striping of vair, and he put this robe about the shoulders of another. Alfgar took from his fair head the holy crown of Ecben: the kingship over all Ecben was his who wore that crown which Alfgar now placed upon the head of another. Alfgar raised toward his lips the hands of Ettaine, he touched for the last time in his life the lovely body of Ettaine, because of whose comeliness the heart of Alfgar had known no peace now for four years; and he placed her right hand in the right hand of another. Then Alfgar knelt, he placed his own hands between the hairy thighs of Ulf, he touched the huge virility of Ulf, and Alfgar swore his fealty and his service to the wearer of the holy crown of Ecben.

It was then that, after a moment of human surprise, Ulf spoke as became a king. But first he waved back the four masked men as they advanced to perform the duties of their office upon the body of Alfgar. The barons murmured a little at that, and the archbishop of Ecben perforce shook his head in unwilling disapproval.

Nevertheless, Ulf pardoned the late treasonable

practices of the fallen rebel now at his feet. Ulf cried a sparing of the thrice forfeited life of Alfgar, and Ulf cried, too, the King's sentence of eternal exile. Then Ulf said heavily, —

" And do you for the future, my man, go your wit-stricken ways in more salutary fear of the King of Rorn — "

" And of Ecben also, sire," remarked the archbishop.

Ulf said: " And of Ecben also! Moreover, do you go your ways, my man, in even livelier fear of the three gods of Rorn, who have within this hour, and in this place, defeated your wicked endeavors, and who will by and by be requiting your disrespectfulness toward their Sending."

The barons cried loyally, " What the king wishes, the law wills!"

But young Alfgar replied: " My king has spoken; and all kings, and all gods also, are honorable in their degree. Yet it is the way of Ecben to serve only one god, and one king, and one lady in domnei. And from that way I shall never depart."

CHAPTER FIVE

The Way of Ulf

CHAPTER FIVE

The Way of Ulf

T HEN was held the marriage feast of Ettaine, the most beautiful of all the women
of this world, who upon that day rewarded handsomely the unexampled heroism and the superb
ideals of those men of Rorn who had died because
of her color and her shaping. She rewarded all
these deceased patriots by crowning their beloved
cause with victory, now that Ettaine became the
wife of Ulf and the Queen over Rorn and Ecben.

But first the altar of the god of Ecben had been
overturned by Ulf's orders, and to the gods of
Rorn was paid that reverence which they required.
To Kuri the men of Ecben offered the proper por-
tions of a shepherd boy and of a red he-goat, and
in honor of Uwardowa they disposed of a white
bull, and to Kogi they gave piecemeal a young
virgin without any fault in her body or in her
repute, in the old way that was pleasing to Kogi.

37

Thus generously did Ulf forgive that ruining which had been sent against him in vain by the three gods of Rorn, because, after all, as the King remarked, they were his gods, and his cousins too. Nobody should look to see unfailing tact displayed by one's cousins. And for the rest, these gods would by and by requite, in an appropriately painful fashion, the rashness of the misguided person who had during that morning interfered with their divine Sending. Ulf, for his own part, preferred to leave that impious Alfgar to the discretionary powers of an offended pantheon. Ulf desired only that — within, of course, the proper limits, and in due consonance with the laws at large and with the various civic regulations of Ecben, — the will of Heaven should be done everywhere.

One need say no more, King Ulf continued, as to a topic so distasteful. Secure in their heritage of noble character and business ability and high moral standards, blessed with a fertile soil and an abundance of natural water-power, the patriots of Ecben would now press forward to put their shoulders to the plow and to free the ship of state from the ashes and overwrought emotions of war. The most liberal policies would be adopted by a monarch whose one aim was to be regarded as the servant of his people; immigration and the investment of foreign capital would be encouraged in every suitable manner; the cultural aspects of life would not be neglected, but, rather, broadened to include interest in all the arts and sciences and manufacturing enterprises generally. Taxes would for the present, and as a purely temporary measure, be quadrupled, now that the nation was privileged to face this supreme hour, this hour wherein to capitalize, for the benefit of oncoming ages, the united energy and integrity and resourcefulness of all Ecben, but not an hour, in the opinion of the speaker, wherein the fate of a misguided and disreputable exile was any longer a really vital issue.

Thus spoke King Ulf from his tall throne builded of apple-wood with rivets of copper.

"His majesty," replied the barons of Ecben, "speaks as a king should; and we of Ecben are well rid of an unbeliever who has offered any such affront to our most holy and excellent gods."

39

" In fact, the man's attitude toward religious matters was always dubious, where his morals were, alas, but too well known," remarked the late archbishop of Ecben, as he hastily put on the robes of the high priest of Kuri.

And Ettaine bent toward her husband fondly. All happiness adorned Ettaine: she was as fair and merry as sunlight upon the sea: you saw that Ettaine was the most beautiful of all the women of this world.

" Delight of both my eyes," said Queen Ettaine, " you speak as a king should. And, as for that Alfgar — ! " A shrug rounded off her exact opinion.

PART TWO

Of Alfgar in His Journeying

*" Loyalty is a Fine Jewel; yet Many that
Wear it Die Beggars."*

CHAPTER SIX

We Come to Darvan

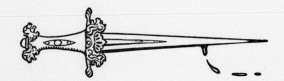

CHAPTER SIX

We Come to Darvan

I T IS told that young Alfgar fared alone to the
dark wood of Darvan. This was an unwholesome place into which, of their own accord, entered
few persons whose intentions were philanthropic:
yet Alfgar journeyed toward Darvan now that
the summoning of Ettarre had led him out of the
set ways of life. And it is told also that under the
outermost trees of this forest sat a leper wrapped
about with an old yellow robe so that his face
might not be seen. Beside him, to the left side of
this leper, was grazing a red he-goat.

This leper rang a little bell, and he cried out,
" Hail, brother! and do you give me now a proper
gift in the king's name."

" There are many kings," said Alfgar, " and
the most of them are no very notable creatures.
Yet in so far that a king is royal, a dream rules in

45

his heart: so must each king of men serve one or another dream which is not known to lesser persons."

" Do you give me my asking, then," the leper replied, with a dryness suited to his more practical trend of thought, " in the name of Ulf, that is King over Rorn and Ecben. For my hands are frail; they are wasted with my disease: and I cannot do all the destroying I desire."

Alfgar said to this leper: " Ulf is but a little king, whom my cunning overthrew at Strathgor, and whom my pleasure raised up again in Ecben. Yet Ulf is royal, in that he would not forsake his gods, for all that they had forsaken him. Moreover, Ulf is my king now. And therefore I may not deny you."

So then the leper told his asking, and for the moment Alfgar seemed unpleased. But he smiled by and by; and, in that grave and lordly manner of his, which merely rational persons found unendurable, young Alfgar said:

" To you that ask in my king's name I must give perforce your asking. For I will not depart from the old way of Ecben. And besides, my

46

hands have touched the hands of Ettarre, and in the touch of sword-hilts and of sceptres and of money bags there is no longer any delight."

The leper then touched Alfgar's hands, and straightway they were frail and shriveled. They became as the hands of an aged person. They shook with palsy, and all strength was gone out of the hands which had made an end of many warriors in the noisy press of battle.

Then yet another queer thing happened upon the edge of the wood of Darvan. It was that Ettaine and Ulf, and all the lords that yesterday had served King Alfgar, and all the houses and the towers of Tagd and Sorram and Pen Loegyr, and of every other town which was in Ecben, now passed by this unwholesome place in the seeming of brightly colored mists. And Alfgar wondered if these matters had ever been true matters, or if all the things which Alfgar had known in the days of his wealth and hardihood were only a part of some ancient dreaming. But the leper put off his yellow robe, and in the likeness of a very old, lean man he pursued these mists and tore and scattered them with strong hands.

47

CHAPTER SEVEN

"The King Pays!"

CHAPTER SEVEN

"The King Pays!"

S O WAS it Alfgar gave that which was asked
in his king's name, and the fallen champion
passed as a weakling into the dark wood, and
came near to the fires which burned in Darvan.
They that dwelt there then swarmed about him,
squeaking merrily, —

" The King pays! "

To every side you saw trapped kings in their
torment, well lighted by the sputtering small fires
of their torment, so that you saw each king was
crowned and proud and silent. And to every side
you saw the little people of Darvan inflicting all
the democratic infamies which their malice could
devise against these persons who had dared to be
royal.

Alfgar went down beneath a smothering
cluster of slender and hairy bodies, smelling of

old urine, which leapt and cluttered everywhere about him, scrambling the one over another like playful rats. He could do nothing with the frail hands which the leper had given him, nor indeed could the might of any champion avail against the people of Darvan when they had squeaked, —

" The King pays! "

Then the trapped kings also cried out to him, with human voices:

" Have courage, brother! Our foes are little, but envy makes them very strong and without either fear or shame when they have scented that which is royal. There is no power upon earth which can withstand the little people of Darvan when once they have raised their hunting-cry, ' The King pays! ' Have courage, brother! for time delivers all kings of men into the power of the little people of Darvan. It is great agony which they put upon us, and from all that which is mortal in us they get their mirth, filthily. But do you have courage, brother, for to that dream which rules in our hearts they may not attain, nor may they vex that dream; even the nature of that dream evades them; they may not ever comprehend or

defile that very small, pure gleam of majesty
which has caused us royal persons to be other than
they are: and it is this knowledge which maddens
the little people of Darvan. So do you have courage, as all we have courage! "

Meanwhile the little people of Darvan were
getting their sport with Alfgar in disastrous ways.
It is not possible to tell of that which was done
to him, for they were an ingenious race. Yet he
came through the wood alive, because upon him
was the mark of the witch-woman whose magic
is more strong than is that magic of time which
betrays all kings of men into the power of the
little people of Darvan.

So he came through that wood yet living. But
behind Alfgar those kings of men that were his
peers remained secure in the dark paradise of
envy, and the little people of Darvan attended to
all their needs.

Such faithful service did this little people render
very gladly to every king, because of envy: which,
with not ever failing charity, endows the most
weak with nimbleness and venom, as though,
through the keen magic of envy, the sluggish,

naked, and defenceless earthworm had become a quick serpent; and which is long-suffering in the while that, like a cunning sapper, it undermines the ways of the exalted; and which builds aspiringly, beyond the dreams of any mortal architect, its bedazzling edifices of falsehood, very quaintly adorned with small gargoyles of unpleasant truths, and sees to it, too, that the imposing structure is well lighted everywhere with malign wit and comfortably heated with moral indignation; and which is a most learned scholar that writes the biographies of the brave, and is openhanded to reward the faithful also with lewd epitaphs; and which, with a noble patience, follows after its prey more steadfastly than any hound pursues its prey; and which piously deludes the over-pious, alike in mosques and in chapels and in synagogues and in pagodas, with a cordial faith that all their betters are by very much their inferiors, if but the truth were known; and which is more eloquent than any angel to deride the truth; and which pleasantly seasons gossip; and which, with its consoling droll whisper, colors the more permanent misfortunes of our kindred and nearer intimates with agreeability; and which weaves, with kinglike opulence, about all kings of men its luxuriant and gross mythology, of drunkenness and theft and lust; and which handsomely enlivens every gathering so often as envy appears under some one of those lesser titles such as this monarch over-modestly affects when envy goes incognito among mankind as zeal, or as candor, or as moral duty; and which yet retained in Darvan its dark paradise, wherein envy ruled without any check or concealment, and wherein the kings of men paid a fit toll to the king of passions for every sort of high endeavor.

CHAPTER EIGHT

We Approach Clioth

CHAPTER EIGHT

We Approach Clioth

A T CLIOTH, just beside the cave, sat a leper wrapped in an old red robe which hid his face. Beside him, to the right-hand side of this leper, lay a large white bull chewing massively at its cud: and this leper rang a little bell when he saw Alfgar.

" Hail, brother! " cried the leper: " and do you give me now a proper gift, in a god's name, before your many wounds have made an end of you."

" There are more gods set over man than I have hurts in my frail body," said Alfgar. " And it may be that no one of these gods is in all ways divine. Yet is each hallowed by the love of his worshippers: and in the hearts of his worshippers each god has kindled a small warming fire of faith and of enduring hope. For that reason should every god be held honorable in his degree."

59

" Why, to be sure! " the leper replied. " Nevertheless, you did not hold honorable the gods of Rorn. And, besides, I cry to you in the name of the god of Ecben."

" He is but a little god, a well-nigh forgotten god," said Alfgar. " I retain no longer any faith in him, and that hope which he kindled is dead a great while since. Yet this god also is made holy by the love of his worshippers, whom I too loved. This god who has gone out of my mind keeps, none the less, his shrine in my deep heart. So in his name I grant your asking."

" Do you give me, then," said the leper, " those golden rings which glitter in your ears."

" Very willingly," said Alfgar, for it seemed to him this was light toll.

But now the white bull lowed: and the leper nodded his veiled head as though in assent.

" — Only, now that I think of it," said the leper, " I must ask for more than those two gold rings. For my own ears, as you can observe, are not pierced: and unless I have pierced ears, then those rings will be of no use to me."

Alfgar saw that this was wholly logical; and

60

yet this logic did not please him. Nevertheless, when the leper had told all his asking, Alfgar replied:

" I may not deny you that which is asked in the name of my own god, to whom I owe all homage except the homage of belief; and I grant your asking. Moreover, I have heard the music of Ettarre, and I wish to keep in my memory only the music of Ettarre, and I would not have it marred by my hearing any other noises."

So the leper touched the ears of Alfgar with strong hands, and the outcast King went down into the cave of Clioth. Then the leper rose, and put off his red robe, and in the likeness of a very old, lean man he went away to resume that labor which has not any ending.

CHAPTER NINE

The Way of Worship

CHAPTER NINE

The Way of Worship

THE tale says then that in the cave of Clioth was not absolute darkness, but, instead, a dim blue glowing everywhere, as though the gleam of decay were intermingled here with the gleam of moonshine. Upon both sides of the cave showed a long row of crumbling altars; and every altar was inscribed with the device of one or another god.

Thus upon the first altar that Alfgar came to was engraved: " I am the Well-doer. I only am the Lord of the two horns, the Governor of all living, and the Conqueror of every land." But upon the next altar you read: " I am the Beneficent. I ordained created things from the beginning. There is no other god save me, who am the giver of winds to all nostrils, and the bestower of delight and ruin to every kind."

The device upon an altar of square-hewn granite said: "I am that I am. I am a jealous god: my thoughts are tempests. Thou shalt have no other god before me." Yet upon an altar of green malachite carved with four skulls was written: "I am the Warrior, the far-darting Slayer of all life and the Slayer of death also. No other god is my peer: through me the sun is risen, and I alone reign over the place where all roads meet."

Such were the devices upon these altars, and upon yet other altars showed yet other devices, but no living man might say to what gods any of these altars had been erected, for all these gods had long ago passed down into Antan. And about each of these altars yet knelt the ghosts of the dead, still worshipping where no god was, because in every age is born, to the troubling of that age, a man, or it may be two men, who will not forsake their gods.

So in that dim blue gleaming did Alfgar come to the ruined altar of the god of Ecben. He knelt there, among ghosts of all which once had been most dear to Alfgar. Beside him knelt his sister Gudrun, who had died when they both were

children. Hilda also was there, and young Game-
lyn. Yonder knelt Alfgar's father — superb and
slightly dull-witted, and more great-hearted than
any person was nowadays, — punctiliously intent
upon his religious duties, as became a properly
reared monarch of the old school. And beside
the father of Alfgar that long-dead queen who
had been Alfgar's mother now turned toward her
son that proud and tender gazing which he so
well remembered. But she did not remember.
There was no recognition in the eyes of Alfgar's
mother as she seemed to look beyond and through
that Alfgar who was not any longer the King of
Ecben, but only an aging vagabond upon whom
was the mark of the witch-woman.

And a vague host of other persons whom he
had known and loved, at Sorram and at Tagd,
when Alfgar was but a boy, knelt there in a blue
gleaming. But all were waving pale phantoms,
and no one of them appeared aware of Alfgar.
These ghosts all gazed beyond and through him,
as though he too were a ghost, in the while that
they worshipped. Thus did they all keep faith,

unthriftily, with that god who now had no gifts for his faithful, and who could no longer aid them, and whom no living person honored any more save only Alfgar, who knew over well that he knelt among the dead to honor a dead god.

"O little god of Ecben," Alfgar said, "it is right that I should bring to you an unthrifty giving of pity and of love and of all reverence. It is needful that I should not forsake you. It is very certain that in no quarter of this earth may I find any god whom I can serve true-heartedly save you alone. . . . For to the North reigns Odin; Zeus triumphs in the South; and Siva holds the East. To the West rule Kuri and Uwardowa, and Kogi also, who are Three in One. And the power of these gods is known, where your forever ended power is not known any longer, and where your name is forgotten."

Then Alfgar said:

"It is known that Odin dwells in the North, at Gladsheim, under a roof of silver, in a fair grove wherein the foliage of each tree is golden. All that which has been or will ever be is revealed to Odin, for this god has drunk, from out of a bronze kettle, the blood of a dwarf intermingled with rum and honey. Therefore does Odin govern all things, and the other gods of the North obey him as their father. He has nine and forty names, and under each name a nation prays to him. The power of Odin is supreme. . . . And it is known that Zeus holds Olympos in the South. He carries in his hand a thunderbolt, and an eagle attends him. The other gods of the South obey him as their father. The young women of the South obey him also, and he begets upon them heroes, but his heart is given to the boy Ganymede."

After that, Alfgar said:

" Ganymede and yet other boys obey this Zeus. He is worshipped in the form of a ram because of his not ever tiring lustiness in all natures of love. In fornication, as in all other matters, the power of Zeus is supreme. . . . And it is known also that in the East three-headed Siva has reared his dwelling place among broad shining pools of water in which grow red and blue and white lotus flowers. He rules there, seated upon a tiger's skin, upon a throne as glorious as is the midday sun. The other gods of the East obey this Siva as their father. Yet whensoever it pleases him to do so, three-headed Siva descends from the brightness and the fragrance of his heaven to run howling about this earth in the appearance of a naked madman, besmeared with ashes and attended by starved demons and gray ghosts, for the power of Siva is supreme. . . . These things are known to all the pious that thrive in the North and in the South and in the East."

And Alfgar said also:

"But in the West, in my own West, it is known that the gods of Rorn have taken their rule over Ecben. From green Pen Loegyr to the gaunt dear hills of Tagd, where once a boy lived in fond sheltered happiness, the power of these three is supreme. Where once you reigned, O little god of Ecben, now these three reign, and they have all honor. The burning of much incense blinds them; the men of Ecben bring to them red he-goats and white bulls and virgins; the needs of these three gods are duly served where your name is not remembered. . . . These things are known.

The Way of Worship

These things are known to every person, O little god of Ecben! But it is not known, O very dear, dead Lord, in what hour and in what place the power went out of you, nor in what tomb you sleep discrowned and forgotten. O little god of Ecben, whom no other man remembers any longer, my pity and fond reverence, and my great love also, now go a-questing after you through the darkness of your unknown grave."

It was in this fashion that, in the faith-haunted cave of Clioth, Alfgar worshipped unthriftily the dead god of Ecben.

Now came toward Alfgar seven creatures having the appearance of jackals, save that each one of them wore spectacles. Such were they whose allotted work it was to discourage the worship of dead gods. Each raised a leg against the altar of the god of Ecben.

When they had finished with that task, these seven remarked, because of their sturdy common-sense:

" This man attempts to preserve the sentiments of Ecben without any of the belief which begot them. This man yet kneels before an altar which his own folly has dishonored, and he yet clings to that god in whom he retains no faith."

After that they carried Alfgar far deeper down into the cave of Clioth: and quietly, in entire darkness, they dealt with him as was their duty. But his life they spared, by howsoever little, and howsoever unwillingly, because upon this aging and frail wanderer they found the mark of the witch-woman whose magic is more strong than is that magic of time which overthrows the altar of every god.

CHAPTER TEN

The Last Giving

CHAPTER TEN

The Last Giving

NOW at the farther end of the cave of Clioth you came again into gray daylight and to a leper who waited there in a black robe, which hid his face, but did not hide the glittering of the gold rings which hung in this leper's ears.

A flock of small birds arose from the dead grass about his feet, and flew away with many swirls and cheepings: you saw that they were swallows. A dark snake glided out from between his feet, and flickeringly passed down into the cave of Clioth, now that this leper rang a little bell.

"Hail, brother!" cried the leper; "and do you give me now a proper gift in your lady's name, before your feebleness and your wounds, and your great age also, have quite done with their thriving work."

"I once had more of ladies than I had of ills," replied Alfgar, "in the fine days when I was the darling of the women of Ecben, and there was not any summoning yet put upon me. For in that far-off season it was I who summoned. I summoned with the frank gaze of a king who does not need to speak his desire: and out of hand a blush and a bridling answered me. So there was Cathra, and Olwen, and Guen, and Hrefna, and Astrid also; there was Lliach of the Bright Breast, and there was Una that was queen over the War Women of Mel; and there were yet others, before the coming of Ettaine. To each of these dear maids my heart was given at one time or another time: and in return they did not deny me their lips."

The leper said, " Nevertheless — "

" To many ladies of romance and of legend," Alfgar continued, now that his mind was upon this matter, " has my heart been given likewise; and those queens who ruled most notably in the world's youth have ruled also in my heart, because it is the way of Ecben to know that every woman is holy and more fine than a man may ever be — "

To that the leper answered, without any doubtfulness, " Stuff and nonsense! "

76

" — And moreover," Alfgar said, with the quiet pertinacity of an aged person, " it is the way of youth to desire that which cannot ever be attained."

" These reflections appear as handsome as they are irrelevant," the leper returned. " Now that you have done with your interminable and very foolish talking, I cry to you for my proper gift, in the name of no harem, but in the name of Ettarre."

" And in that that most dear name," said Alfgar, " I grant all askings."

So then the leper told his asking, and Alfgar sighed. Yet, in that grave and lordly manner of his, which merely rational persons found unendurable, decrepit Alfgar said:

" I will not depart from the old way of Ecben. Therefore I may not deny to anybody that which is asked in the name of my lady in domnei. And indeed, it may be that I shall make shift well enough, even so. For I have seen the face of Ettarre, and I desire only to retain my loyal memories of that beauty which had in it not any flaw."

The leper replied, " Loyalty is a fine jewel; yet many that wear it die beggars."

Then the leper touched the eyes of Alfgar, and Alfgar fared onward upon a gray and windy way. But the leper arose, and put off his black robe, and from behind the rock upon which he had been sitting he took up the most sharp of scythes and the oldest of all hour glasses.

CHAPTER ELEVEN

How Time Passed

CHAPTER ELEVEN

How Time Passed

THEN this very old, lean man cried out " Oho! " and yet again he cried " Oho! " and, after that, he went away chuckling, and saying to himself:

" I have well repaired the hurt honor of the gods of Rorn. I have well dealt with this Alfgar who, because of his fond notions, has yielded up to me willingly that which other men give perforce. For I take this toll from all. There is no youth which I do not lead into corruption; there is no loveliness but becomes my pillage; and man's magnanimity begets no bustlings which I do not quiet by and by. I chill faith. I teach hope to deride itself. I parch charity. The strong cities, which withstand the battalions and the arbalests and the scaling ladders, may not withstand me. I play with kingdoms. Oho, but I play with every kingdom as

I played with Atlantis and with Chaldea and with Carthage and with Troy. I break my playthings. I ignore neither the duke nor the plowman. All withers under my touch, and is not any longer remembered anywhere upon earth."

After that the old man said:

"The earth itself I waste away into a cinder adrift in that wind which fans the flickering of the stars. I know this assuredly, for my skill is proved, and in heaven I keep always before me the cold, quiet moon as a model of what I mean to make of this earth. Oho, and in heaven also, all gods observe me with the alert eyes which rabbits turn toward the hound who is not yet upon their scent. They know that I alone exalt the Heavenly Ones, and that for some while I humor them, as I to-day have humored the vexed minds of the gods of Rorn. Yet these Heavenly Ones well know what in the end I make of their omnipotence. Let Kuri and Uwardowa, and Kogi also, have a care of my industry! The road behind me is littered with despoiled temples. The majesty of many gods is the dust in that roadway."

And this very old, lean man said likewise:

" But the road before me, oho, but the road before me, is obscure. Its goal is not known. If there be any power above me, it is not known. If there be any purpose anywhere in my all-ruining labor, it is not known. Yet if that power exists, and if that purpose and that goal be set, I pray that these may end my endless laboring by and by, for I am old and tired, and there is no joy to be got out of my laboring."

PART THREE

Of Alfgar in the Grayness

*" The Touch of Time does More than
the Club of Hercules."*

CHAPTER TWELVE

The Way of All Women

CHAPTER TWELVE

The Way of All Women

I T IS told that infirm old Alfgar passed on a
gray road beneath gray skies, and about him
blew that wind which fans the flickering of the
stars. The first woman that he met there was gray
and fat as a fed coffin worm. She mumbled, between toothless gums, —

"Tarry! for I am that Cathra who was your
first love."

And it is told also that the second woman he met
was gray and lean. A piping voice came out of her
lank quivering jaws, and that voice said, —

"Tarry! for I am Olwen whom you loved with
your whole heart."

Then Hrefna, and Guen, and Lliach, and
Astrid, and Una, and all the other most dear maids
that Alfgar had followed after in his youth, cried
out their willingness to reward his love. Ettaine

came also, bent and infirm and gray; her withered hands trembled, and her guts rumbled rattlingly, in the while that Ettaine was saying, —

" Tarry, delight of both my eyes! "

For youth had long ago gone out of these maidens; the years had pilfered their sweet colorings; and time had so nibbled away every part of their comeliness, that these were but gray and decayed old harridans who leered and cackled and broke wind as each plucked at Alfgar's ragged sleeve in the windy grayness.

The gaunt tall King trudged onward.

But here, the gray way was littered to the right hand and to the left hand with a scattering of papers which flutteringly rose up in the persistent wind, and these also spoke with Alfgar.

" Tarry! for I am Oriana, the most faithful and most fair of all women," was the first thin whispering that the old King heard: " but Amadis is far from this place, so let us now take our glad fill of love."

Then another paper rustled: " I am Aude. Roland loved me until his death, and it was of

Roland's death that I died; but for your dear love's sake I live again."

And a third paper lisped: "I am Yseult, Mark's queen. But I loved a harper, and the music of this Tristram made all my life a music. Not even death might still that music, for our names endure as one song that answers to another song. But Alfgar now is my one love."

He saw then that upon these papers were very crudely drawn the figures of women, in old and faded colors, and he so knew that he was being wooed by the fairest ladies of romance and of legend. But these swept about him futilely, adrift in the wind which fans the flickering of the stars: and all these paper figures were smutched with the thumb marks and the fly droppings and the dim grime of uncountable years. So did they pass as tatterings of soiled, splotched paper in which time had left no magic and no warmth and no beauty.

Alfgar sighed: but he went onward.

Then very many skeletons came crying out to Alfgar. And the first skeleton said:

"Tarry! for I am Cleopatra. I am that one

Cleopatra whose name yet lives. All the large world lay in this little hand, as my plaything. I ruled the South and North: and I ruled merrily, as became the daughter of Rā, the Lord of Crowns, and the well beloved of Amen-Rā, the Lord of the Throne of the Two Lands. The war drums and the shoutings of the legions under their tall crests of red horsehair could not prevail against the sweetness of my laughter: with one kiss I conquered Cæsar, and all his army. Then Antony brought me new kingdoms, and with each of these, and with him also, I played as I desired, at the price of yet another kiss. But my third lover was more wise and cold than were these Roman captains, and yet I died of his kissing, because that dusty-colored, horned worm was too fiercely enamored of my loveliness."

The gaunt tall King trudged onward.

But another skeleton cried out: "Nay, do you tarry instead with me. For I am that Magdalene whose body was as a well builded market-place wherefrom men got all their desires. My love was very liberal: my love was a highway whereupon glad armies marched in triumph: my love

was a not ever ending festival where new guests
come and go. Then a god passed, saying, 'Love
ye one another.' But I stayed perverse, for after
that time I loved him alone. In the hour of his
tortured dying I did not leave him: when he
returned from death I, and I only, awaited him,
at the door of the gray tomb, at dawn, beneath
the olive-trees, where the birds chattered with a
surprising sweetness. But his voice was more
sweet than theirs. Whithersoever he went, there
I too must be: and for that reason he was followed
by many who were enamored of my loveliness."

Alfgar sighed: but he went onward.

Then yet a third skeleton said: " It were far
better that you should tarry with me. For I am
Balkis; Sheba bore me, from out of the womb of
an antelope; and in all the ways of love I am well
skilled. My skill was spoken of throughout the
happy land between Negrân and Ocelis. King
Scharabel chose me to be his queen because of
that fine skill I had; and I rewarded him with a
sharp troth-plighting. With one dagger thrust I
took from him his kingdom and his life also. But
it was in a bed builded of gold and carved with

triangles that I conquered yet another king, when Solomon shaved from my legs three hairs, and I bereft him of his over-famous wisdom. So did he worship Eblis and Milcom after that midnight, because I served these gods very wantonly in their high places, and the old lewd itching Jew was enamored of my loveliness."

But Alfgar put aside the lipless mouth, and all the other mouldering cold bones, of wise Balkis, also.

In such fashion did these skeletons, and yet other grinning small skeletons, flock after the tall wanderer and cry out to him. The sweetings of Greece and of Almayne and of Persia foregathered in that endless grayness with the proud whores of the Merovingians and of the Pharaohs, and each of these luxurious women wooed Alfgar. The empresses of Rome and of Byzantium came likewise: the czarinas of Muscovy and the sultanas of Arabia also attended him. The head-wives of the Caziques and of the Incas, the nieces of the Popes, and the maharanees of the Great Khans, all flocked about King Alfgar: and all were mouldy bones, in their torn and rotted gravecloths. Then from the mire along the gray roadway arose the voices of the queens of Assyria and of Babylon, who now were scattered dust and horse dung. All these, whom time had done with, now cried out wooingly to Alfgar.

But infirm old Alfgar went onward without heeding any of them, for so strong was the magic which Ettarre had put upon him that all these who were the fairest of the women of this world no longer seemed desirable.

CHAPTER THIRTEEN

What a Boy Thought

CHAPTER THIRTEEN

What a Boy Thought

AT THE gate of the garden, beside the lingham post which stood there in eternal erection, sat a young boy who was diverting himself by whittling, with a small green-handled knife, a bit of cedar-wood into the quaint shaping which that post had. His hair was darkly red: and now, as he regarded Alfgar with brown and wide-set eyes, the face of this boy was humorously grave, and he nodded now, as the complacent artist nods who looks upon his advancing work and finds all to be near his wishes.

"Time has indeed laid hold of you with both hands," said this boy, "and the touch of time does more than the club of Hercules. It is not the Alfgar who had the pre-eminent name that I am seeing, but only a frail and blinded and deaf vagabond."

"Nevertheless," said Alfgar, and even now he spoke in that grave and lordly manner which once had from a throne annoyed the more human of his hearers, "nevertheless, I have not departed from the old way of Ecben."

"I know that way," the boy replied. "It is a pretty notion to have but one king and one god and, above both of them, one lady. Oh, yes, it is a most diverting notion, and a very potent drug, to believe that these three are holy and all-important. I too have got diversion from that notion, in my day. . . ."

The boy shook his red curls. He said, shruggingly:

"But no toy lasts forever. And out of that notion also time has taken the old nobleness and the fine strength."

Then Alfgar asked, "But what do you do here who wait in this gray place like a sentinel?"

The boy replied: "I do that which I do in every place. Here also, at the gateway of that garden into which time has not yet entered, I fight with time my ever-losing battle, because to do that diverts me."

He smiled: but Alfgar did not smile.

" To be seeking always for diversion, sir," said Alfgar, with a king's frankness, " is but a piddling way of living."

" Ah, but then," the boy answered him, " I fight against the gluttony of time with so many very amusing weapons, — with gestures and with attitudes and with wholly charming phrases; with tears, and with tinsel, and with sugar-coated pills, and with platitudes slightly regilded. Yes, and I fight him also with little mirrors wherein gleam confusedly the corruptions of all lust, and ruddy loyalty, and a bit of moonshine, and the pure diamond of the heart's desire, and the opal cloudings of human compromise: but, above all, I fight that ravening dotard with the might of my own folly."

" I do not understand these foolish sayings," Alfgar returned. " Yet I take you to be that Horvendile who is the eternal playfellow of my lady in domnei — "

" But I," the boy answered, " I take it that I must be the eternal playfellow of time. For piety and common-sense and death are rightfully time's toys; and it is with these three that I divert myself."

Alfgar said: "This also is but a piddling way of talking. I must frankly tell you, Messire Horvendile, if but for your own good, that such frivolousness is very unbecoming in an immortal."

The boy laughed, without any mirth, at this old vagabond's old notions. "Then I must tell you," said Horvendile, "that my immortality has sharp restrictions. For it is at a price that I pass down the years, as yet, in eternal union with the witch-woman whose magic stays — as yet — more strong than is the magic of time. The price is that I only of her lovers may not ever hope to win Ettarre. This merely is permitted me: that I may touch the hand of Ettarre in the moment that I lay that hand in the hand of her last lover. I give, who may not ever take. . . ."

But Horvendile laughed at that, too, still without any gaiety. He then added:

"So do I purchase an eternally unfed desire against which time — as yet — remains powerless."

"But I, sir, go to take my desires, as becomes

an honest chevalier," said Alfgar, resolutely, as the infirm old King now passed beyond this fribbling and insane immortal.

The boy replied to him: " That very well may be. Yet how does that matter, either, — by and by — in a world wherein the saga of every man leads to the same Explicit? "

But Horvendile got no answer to this question, at this season, nor at any other season. So — by and by — he gave this question a fine place among those other platitudes which he had slightly regilded.

PART FOUR

Of Alfgar in a Garden

*" The Gods Provide for Him
that Holds to his Faith."*

CHAPTER FOURTEEN

We Encounter Dawn

CHAPTER FOURTEEN

We Encounter Dawn

IT IS told that all loveliness endured in this garden whereinto time had not yet entered. It is told that, advancing very wearily through the first glow of dawn, Alfgar now passed into the spring of a year which was not registered upon any almanac. Here youth, as always, lived for the passing moment: the difference here was that the moment did not pass. And it is told also that this ever-abiding moment was that moment wherein the spring dawn promises a day more fair than any day may ever be, and when the young leaves whisper in their merry prophesying of more than a century of summers may by any chance fulfil.

But Alfgar was no longer in the prime of his youth. To every side of him, through the first glow of dawn, young persons walked in couples, and they were glad because they knew that the world was their plaything, and that their love was a wholly unexampled love which the dark daughters of Dvalinn, even those three Norns who weave the fate of all the living, regarded respectfully; and which the oncoming years all labored to reward with never-ending famousness and contentment. They, who were young, knew that time was but a bearer of resplendent gifts; they knew that their love was eternal; they knew also that they themselves were far more remarkable and more glorious than any other pair of lovers which had ever existed: and, as they walked there in couples, they mentioned all these facts.

But Alfgar walked alone: and of necessity, he looked at these youngsters with the eyes which time had given him; and it was with the ears which time had given him that he heard these chattering, moonstruck, gangling young half-wits talk their nonsense.

In no great while, however, as the infirm old King reflected, these silly children would be self-respecting men and women, and this bleating and this pawing at one another would happily be put aside for warfare and housework and other sensible matters. Those interlocked young hands would soon be parted, the one hand to kill honorably, with fine sword strokes, in a wellbred mêlée of gentlemen, and the other hand to scrub stewpans and wash diapers. And that would be an excellent outcome: for, to old Alfgar's finding, the unrestrainedness of these semi-public endearments was, in its way, an indignity to human intelligence.

CHAPTER FIFTEEN

How the King Triumphed

How the King Triumphed

THEN Alfgar saw a woman who walked alone, upon a gravelled walkway, beneath the maples and the sycamore-trees of this garden. She came toward the old wanderer, and a jangling and a skirling noise came with her, so that Alfgar knew this was indeed Ettarre. He heard again that music which sought and could not find its desire in any quarter of earth.

But the ears which time had given him got no delight from this music. It seemed, to this decrepit king of men, an adolescent and morbid music. He did not like these unhappy noises which seemed to doubt and question. It was better to have about you much merrier noises than were these noises, in the while that yet remained for an aging frail old fellow to be hearing any noises at all.

She was near him now. And Ettarre, he found, was well enough to look at, but in no way remarkable: for to the eyes which time had given him the face of one woman was very much like that of any other woman. Nevertheless, this was his appointed lady in domnei. So the old romantic knelt, and he kissed the hands of this girl who appeared, after all, quite nice looking, in an unpretentious fashion.

He knelt because this was the Ettarre who had drawn Alfgar out of the set ways of life, and who had stripped him of all that well-thought-of monarchs desired. It was in order that he might kneel here at the feet of his appointed lady in domnei, upon this walkway, — which really was a bit damp, he reflected, for a person of his age, — and upon these rather uncomfortable small stones, that Alfgar had given up his pre-eminent name. It was in order to be hurting his thin old knees, with these little rocks' sharp edges, that he had given up his tall throne builded of apple-wood with rivets of copper, and the King of Ecben's four houses builded of white polished stone, with all their noble furnishings, and their fertile gardens and orchards, and their low-lying, red-roofed stables; and he had given up, too, his big golden sceptre with the five kinds of rubies in it, and his herds of fine speckled cattle at Pen Loegyr, and all the pretty shaping and the bright colors of Ettaine, the daughter of Thordis Bent-Neck.

These things Alfgar had yielded up not all unwillingly, because of his magnanimous old notions. These things he had put far behind him now, so that he might be following after that Ettarre whom a poet fetched from out of the Waste Beyond the Moon, to be alike the derider and the prey and the destroyer of mankind. Of all these things the witch-woman had bereft King Alfgar, and of all other things save only of that dream which yet ruled defiantly in the old wanderer's brave heart.

CHAPTER SIXTEEN

Contentment of a Chevalier

CHAPTER SIXTEEN

Contentment of a Chevalier

T HUS then is the quest ended," Alfgar said, after he had risen up shakily from kneeling upon the edges of those more and yet more uncomfortable small stones. " I have kept faith with the old way of Ecben, and with you also I have kept faith."

The girl answered: " You have kept faith, instead, with Alfgar, after your own fashion, and after no fashion which became a well-thought-of monarch."

Now Alfgar went on speaking with the quiet pertinacity of an old man; and he spoke, too, as though he were a little, but not very deeply, puzzled by a matter of no really grave importance, saying:

" So have I won to you who were my lady in domnei and my heart's desire. But I am aged now, and it is as your playfellow said: time has laid hold of me with both hands, and with the weak remnants of my mortal body's strength I may neither take nor defend you as becomes a king of men. The music that I once delighted in seems only a thin vexing now. And there is in your face no longer any beauty that my wearied eyes can find."

The girl replied: " Yet even from the first, my friend, you followed after a music which you could not hear, and after a shining to which your eyes were dimmed. All that which other men desire you have given up because of a notion in which you did not ever quite believe. Yes: you have clung — in your own fashion, — to the old way of Ecben."

He said, " And for that reason, I am content."

She answered him with that cool, and yet condoning, bright gaze which women keep for the strange notions of men. She answered him with words also, saying:

" Yet so have you raised up a brutish and lewd Ulf to the throne of Ecben. So have you tumbled down the god of Ecben. So have you lost that Ettaine for whom your love was human and convenient to the ways of men. So do you stand here, a very aged outcast, from whom all ecstasy has departed. Thus ends the King of Ecben's questing after his vain dream, in folly and wide hurt."

He replied: "Yet am I content. For I have served that dream which I elected to be serving. It may be that no man is royal, and that no god is divine, and that our mothers and our wives have not any part in holiness. Oh, yes, it very well may be that I have lost honor and applause, and that I take destruction, through following after a dream which has in it no truth. Yet my dream was noble; and its nobility contents me."

To that the girl returned, rather sadly, " Alas, my friend, but it is an imagining at which Heaven laughs; and the gray Norns do not fulfil that dream for any man."

Alfgar replied: " Then men are better than that power which made them. For the kings of men do not laugh at this dream: and in the heart of every person that is royal this dream may be fulfilled even in the while that his body fails and perishes."

" Yet," said Ettarre, " yet, as the strength of a man's mortal body fails, so do his desires perish

also. It is a thing more sad than any other thing
which men know about, that under the touch of
time even they who serve with the most ardor
men's highest fancies must lose, a little by a little,
all hunger and all faith as to that which is beyond
and above them."

He now looked somewhat wistfully into this
girl's quite nicely colored and shaped face which
was, to him, so like the face of any other young
woman who has good health. The gaunt old man
flung back his head. His white hair fluttered about
in the dawn wind, untidily, and the palely colored
eyes of the tricked wanderer had a vexed and tor-
mented shining, in the while that he said:

"It is not a true thing which you are speaking.
For I retain my faith in that which is beyond and
above me. I have lost the desire and the vision: but
I retain my faith. I retain my faith in that beauty
which I may not see, and in that music which I
may not hear ever any more, and in that dream
which has betrayed me. And I am content."

The girl answered: "You are strangely obsti-
nate. And I could never let anyone remain
content."

124

With that she clasped for one moment his withered hands between her hands, and the witch-woman said, very tenderly:

"Most brave and steadfast, and most foolish, of all them who have followed after Ettarre, the gods do well to smile at your strange and fond imaginings. And yet, tall king of men, the gods provide for him that holds to his faith."

She touched his ears. Her finger tips fell lightly upon his wrinkled eyelids.

CHAPTER SEVENTEEN

The Changing of Alfgar

The Changing of Alfgar

ALL things were changed for Alfgar. He was not any longer a frail and aged person, now that contentment had gone out of him. For all his stoical, enforced contentment had now made room for joy, because his youth had returned to him; and in that garden, now, exulted that Alfgar who had been foremost among the champions of Ecben, the Alfgar who had been the most powerful of kings and the most ardent of lovers and the most knightly of chevaliers.

All things were changed for Alfgar. He noted, with roving and imperious young eyes, that lilies abounded to each side of him, and that in this garden many climbing white roses also were lighted by the clear and tempered radiancy of early dawn. White rabbits were frisking about King Alfgar. He saw that all the world was lovely, and that time was friendly to all lovers. He heard a music

which was not of this world, and it still sought
and could not find its desire in any quarter of
earth. But now was intermingled with this music
the sound of doves that called to their mates; and
in this music he found, now, no doubtfulness and
no discontent, but only the dear promise of a life
which presently would be created out of the resist-
less might of this music's yearning, and which
would be more noble than had been any life yet
known to human kind.

All things were changed for Alfgar, who
grasped with strong hands the hands of the most
lovely of the women who are not quite of this
world. For this was visibly that ever-young Ettarre
whom very long ago the magic of a poet's love
and the wizardry of mathematics had fetched
from out of the Waste Beyond the Moon, to be
the delight and the ruin of many human lovers
less fortunate than Alfgar had been, and to elude
them eternally. But Alfgar she could not elude, he
knew, because of those strong hands which held
her hands securely.

" The gods provide," said Alfgar, joyously, " for
him that holds to his faith! "

Changing of Alfgar

So was it that all things were changed for Alf-gar through the touch of the witch-woman who had drawn him out of the set ways of life into the garden between dawn and sunrise, and whose magic is more great than is the magic of time.

CHAPTER EIGHTEEN

As to Another Marriage Feast

CHAPTER EIGHTEEN

As to Another Marriage Feast

FROM all quarters of the garden came the young lovers, two by two, in high rejoicing. They rejoiced because, once more, the gray Norns had regarded respectfully the importance of a sincere love-affair, and because the oncoming years were again laboring to reward the steadfastness of true love with never-ending fame and contentment. They cried aloud to Alfgar, with friendly smiles and with gay caperings, —

" The gods provide for him that holds to his faith! "

Then they all praised Alfgar cordially. Each couple said, indeed, with the most sympathizing kind of politeness, that Alfgar and his appointed lady in domnei were more remarkable and more glorious than any other pair of lovers which had ever existed, saving only one pair, — which pair no couple was so egotistic as to mention outright.

They that had served Ettarre came also, all those maimed poets whose living she had ruined. And they said:

"Hail and farewell, Ettarre! Because of you, we could be contented with no woman. We turned away from that frank and wholesome world wherein frank, wholesome maidens walked amiably along sunlit ways. We perceived that the younger females of our kind were pleasant to the touch and were agreeably tinted. But we turned away, we blundered into more murky places, and we got deep scarrings there, because these maids were not as was that witch-woman whom we had seen and might not forget. As moths flitter after torches, so did we pursue your lost loveliness, to our own hurt."

And these poets said also:

"Because of your music, we could get no delight from the music of our verses nor from any melody that is of this world. We were enamored of a music which no words might entrap nor cage. There was a music which had no fault in it, as we well knew, because we had heard such music once, for too brief a while. But no man who lived upon earth might recapture that music. The cradle-songs of the fond mothers who bore us were less dear than was that music. The pipes and the organs and the fiddles made no such music. We heard the trumpets and the harps and the clarions; we heard the church bells; and we were not comforted."

Then these poets said:

" Because of you, we lived among mankind as exiles. The emperors and the captains perceived that we did not regard their famousness as a weighty matter. The priests and the well-thought-of sages perceived that in the while they instructed us our minds were upon a mystery, and that our thinking cherished a legend which was not their legend. So the strong derided us, and said lightly that we were wit-stricken: but, in their troubled hearts, they hated us. For we went among them as men who had drunk wine from a goblet of fairy gold: the wholesome fare of earth may not content such men: and to all human kind they become abhorrent."

Whereafter these maimed poets cried out very fondly:

" Yet we who never found contentment in any hour of our living, all we who followed after you to our own hurt, we would have nothing changed. That loveliness which we saw once and then lost forever, and that music which we heard just once and might not ever hear again, were things more fine than is contentment. Hail and farewell, Ettarre! "

Such was the speaking of these poets, and so was it that they all made ready for the marriage feast of Alfgar the high king and Ettarre the most fair of those women who are not quite of this world.

The Way It Ended

CHAPTER NINETEEN

The Way It Ended

AND Horvendile came likewise. As he had done in Alfgar's dream, so now did this red-headed boy smile without any mirth; and he laid the hand of Ettarre in the hand of Alfgar, in the while that this boy was speaking a word of power.

Then Alfgar grasped exultingly, with his strong arms, the wife that he had won, and his lips touched her lips. It was in that instant the young face of Horvendile became white and drawn. It is not well to give where one desires.

And in that same instant also the maimed servitors of Ettarre were gone, and all the beautiful and merry young lovers passed in a many-colored mistiness. But to these had succeeded a wonder-working even more amiable, for in this garden three immortals now sat watching over Alfgar friendlily.

The largest of these smiling gods was broad-browed and great-eyed, with very long black hair and a thick beard: the robe he wore was fashioned out of five hundred and forty and three goatskins, and with his left hand he carried a spear of flickering fire. The second god was clothed in red, striped with fine flickering lines of white, and in his yellow hair were two white plumes: between the thumb and the forefinger of his left hand he held a white bull, as yet only partially eaten. But the third god was copper-colored, and he was by so much the least of the divine three that, now he also sat cross-legged upon the ground, his head rose but a little way above the taller locust-trees of the garden. About his head flew swallows. He was naked save that wrapped everywhere around his body was a darkly gleaming snake which whispered into the ear of its master with an ever flickering tongue.

Such were the appearances of Kuri and of Uwardowa and of Kogi, who were the supreme gods of Rorn. And each of them was smiling now that Alfgar had won to his heart's desire. It was a great joy to Alfgar to see that these gods bore toward him no grudge. Instead, each god had lifted up his right hand, in blessing and in forgiveness.

Then these gods arose and went away laughingly. The power was not yet gone out of them.

It was in this way that the garden between dawn and sunrise was emptied of all living creatures save Ettarre and Horvendile, and that at their feet you saw, still faintly simmering, that which the forgiveness of the gods of Rorn had left of King Alfgar.

PART FIVE

Of Horvendile and Ettarre

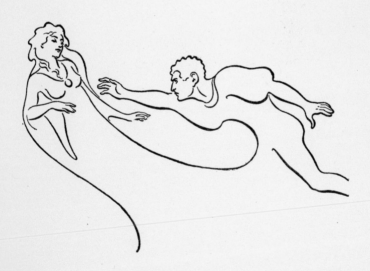

*" Nor do They Get from their
Playing any Joy."*

CHAPTER TWENTY

We Regard Other Wanderers

CHAPTER TWENTY

We Regard Other Wanderers

T HE gods provide for him that holds to his faith," said Horvendile, with a slow smiling. " These jealous and rather pig-headed Heavenly Ones have very smoothly rounded off our playing with this tall, over-faithful fool: and so the saga of King Alfgar, after all, ends neatly enough."

But Ettarre did not smile. " This man was better and more fine than we are. I would that I could weep for this brave outcast king of men whose folly was more noble than is our long playing. . . . Dear Horvendile, and why may you give me no human heart? "

The eternal artist looked very sadly toward her who was the pulse of all his dreams' desire, in the while that she waited there beyond the blackened and ruined body of King Alfgar. " And why may you give me no happiness, Ettarre, such as — in this tall fool's one moment, — we gave to him? "

Thereafter Horvendile parted from the witch-woman, but not for long. For all happiness must end with death, and all that which is human must die. But Horvendile and his Ettarre, who are not either happy nor quite human, may not, their legend tells us, ever die, nor have they yet parted from each other for the last time.

And yet, this legend tells us also, they must live in eternal severance, in that it stays his doom that he only of her lovers may not hope to win Ettarre. In recompense, he may not ever wholly lose her, as must all they who approach too near to the witch-woman lose her eternally, along with all else which they have.

Some say this Horvendile is that same Madoc who first fetched Ettarre from out of the gray Waste Beyond the Moon, to live upon our earth in many bodies. The truth of this report is not certainly known. But it is known that these two pass down the years in a not ever ending severance which is their union. And it is known that in their passing they allure men out of the set ways of life, and so play wildly with the lives of men for their diversion. As they beguiled Alfgar, so have these beguiled a great sad host of other persons upon whom Horvendile and Ettarre have put a summoning for their diversion's sake, lest these two immortals should think too heavily of their own doom.

To those men of whom they get their sport they give at worst one moment of contentment. But Horvendile and his Ettarre have only an unfed desire as they pass down the years together; and because of that knowledge which they share, hope does not travel with them, nor do they get from their playing any joy. For each of these tricked lovers knows that each is but an empty shining, and that, thus, each follows after the derisive shadow of a love which the long years have not made real.

THE COLOPHON CALLED:

"Hail and Farewell, Ettarre!"

" Finis adest rerum."

CHAPTER ONE

Which Disposes of the Witch-Woman

Which Disposes of The Witch-Woman

YOU have heard the cry of aging and maimed poets to the witch-woman as they took their last leave of her. And for one, I find it not unnatural that I here tend to repeat the gist of their observations now that with the ending of King Alfgar's saga I also take my last leave of *The Witch-Women,* which was to have been a book.

It is now a volume which, in its complete form, must remain in John Charteris' library of un-written books. When I most recently visited Fair-haven *The Witch-Woman* stood in very excellent company, between Milton's *King Arthur* and Frances Newman's *History of Sophistication*: and the general appearance of *The Witch-Woman*

then so favorably impressed me that I was at pains to copy out and to preserve at least its Table of Contents.

The Witch-Woman, as I thus found, was to have contained ten fairly lengthy episodes entitled, in their planned order: The Music from Behind the Moon; The Thirty-first of February; The Furry Thing That Sang; The Lean Hands of Volmar; The Holy Man Who Washed; The Little Miracle of St. Lesbia; The White Robe; The Evasions of Ron; The Child Out of Fire; and The Way of Ecben.

For this never written *Witch-Woman* was to have been, in its Intended Edition, a dizain which would have followed through several centuries the adventuring of Ettarre and her immortal *souteneur,* — or, to be wholly accurate, the adventuring of ten lovers of Ettarre who, howsoever differing in other respects, yet one and all committed the grave error of touching, and of striving to possess, the mortal body which at that time Ettarre was wearing. Yet in the final outcome of affairs, through causes hereinafter indicated clearly enough, this intended dizain, now that I

complete *The Way of Ecben,* has dwindled into a mere trilogy concerned with Ettarre and with three attitudes toward human life. . . . I think there is, at this late date, no pressing need for me to name this trinity of attitudes about which I have written so much. Yet, for safety's sake, I shall formally point out here that *The Music from Behind the Moon* is about Ettarre and the poet Madoc (who may or who may not have been called Horvendile after the losing of his wealth, his wife, and his wits also), and that *The White Robe* deals with Ettarre and a Bishop of Valnères who was notably gallant. In logic, therefore, when I found it was permitted me to complete but one more of the eight unfinished stories about Ettarre, I elected to write out *The Way of Ecben,* which, as you have seen, treats of Ettarre and of an Alfgar who was, above all, chivalrous.

Moreover, this story of *The Way of Ecben* had the advantage of suggesting in itself, I thought, at least some of the reasons why there should now be no more books about Poictesme or Lichfield, or about any more of the inheritors of Dom Manuel's life, — of which life all my books up to this date have been a biography. For the touch of time, about the effects of which you have but now been reading, with a king as protagonist, does not spare writers either. The uncharitable may even assert that *The Way of Ecben* quite proves this fact. In any case, now that the units of the long Biography of Dom Manuel's life add up to a neat twenty which is convenient to the laws of Poictesme, and now that with a yet more coercive arithmetic the years of my own living add up to fifty, *The Way of Ecben* has appeared to its writer a thesis wholly fit to commemorate my graduation from, and my eternal leave-taking of, the younger generation, alike in life and in letters.

CHAPTER TWO

Which Takes Up an Unprofitable Subject

CHAPTER TWO

Which Takes Up an Unprofitable
Subject

I APPROACH thus unavoidably a theme which nobody can approach with any real profit. I mean, the younger generation. I mean that the conduct of the younger generation is a topic concerning which the sole possible verdict to be rendered from the more sedate side of forty was long ago fixed by adamantean usage.

To such time-ripened judgment the activities of the younger generation have always, without any exception, been a sign of world-wide degeneracy ever since these activities provoked the Deluge, and brought about the decadence of Rome — *ætas parentum tulit nos nequiores,* you may find Horace lamenting at, quaintly enough, about the time of Christ's birth, — and enraged

163

Dante, and upset John Milton into reams of mar-
moreal blank verse, and, at a slightly later period,
aggrieved the Old Woman who Lived in a Shoe.

From the beginning, it would seem, all really
matured opinion has been at one on the point that
the younger generation was speeding posthaste
to the dogs. Since the commencement of recorded
literature, in any event, full proof has not been
lacking that oldsters everywhere in every era have
drawn a snarling comfort from this pronounce-
ment just as pertinaciously, and just as pathetically,
as the world's current youth has always been posi-
tive that, once everybody over fifty was disposed
of, the human race was bound for the millennium
around the next corner but one.

In practice, though, the younger generation appears invariably to get to middle age before it does
to either the dogs or the millennium; and then of
course replaces the fallacies of youth with such
substitutes for logic as middle age finds acceptable
whensoever it discourses as to yet another pestifer-
ous younger generation.

Of middle age I intend to speak later. Meanwhile, so far as I may conjecture, the younger

generation has always passed through its so brief
career in a never failing excitement, — an excitement roused by the discovery that the existence of
God is open to dispute, but that the pleasures of
coition are not.

I can well recall that in my own Victorian first
heyday these facts were known. They were not,
to be sure, very often encountered in print: but
in the conversation of the young, and especially in,
as it were, co-educational tête-à-têtes, I am afraid
that no themes were more familiar.

No, I really cannot remember that in my late-
Victorian boyhood (McKinley being Consul),
young persons when left to themselves were over-
rigorously hampered either in speech or action.
Certain words one avoided: but all these had many
synonyms, apart from the fact that the things
they stood for could be, and were, made livelily
communicative in pantomime. In brief, all our
unlegalized and callow, but consummated, amours
were conducted with a civil furtiveness, yet without, in the last outcome, demanding any strenuous
and time-taxing amount of concealment.

One found, instead, that society at large was

here, in a benevolent, slightly flustered way, intent to ignore what was plain enough. Approaching points a bit more delicate, and entering now in reverie the Rooseveltian era, one found that intelligent husbands and intelligent parents had every logical reason to avoid publicity for all such discoveries as they, in either capacity, would particularly deplore. It followed that the Rooseveltian husband, or the Rooseveltian parent, whensoever visited by unavoidable suspicions, was at polite pains not to verify them. . . . So the younger generation of those days was more quiet than are its current successors: but I cannot assert that, beneath this relative quietness, it was any the less sophisticated, nor that it sacrificed upon the altars of respectability any undue amount of carnal indulgence.

Which Touches Youth and Uncrabbéd Age

CHAPTER THREE

Which Touches Youth and Uncrabbéd Age

I INCLINE, in short, to think that in human economy the younger generation has always remained a tolerably staple product. Its language varies, as does also perhaps, at times, the pitch of its voice: but its theme does not vary. Its age-old theme is, always, a restatement of the truism that its elders have lied about most matters, and have mismanaged all matters, beyond human endurance. And its mistake is — always — to believe that the lying and the mismanagement may by and by be remedied.

For youth, to the one side, has faith and hope. But middle age tends rather to dismiss these two cardinal virtues in favor of charity. Youth, in a less happy aspect, is heir to the superior pleasures of pessimism, and to the warm gustos of moral indignation: but middle age has mastered that invaluable gesture which is known as a shrug.

Meanwhile, until forty-five or thereabouts, no man has any first-hand knowledge as to the average of human life, through the sufficing reason that he has seen but tatters and small scattered segments of the affair. At forty-five, though, he has watched his own thinned generation straggle into maturity, and the generation of his parents filed away in caskets. Old age still remains to be endured — perhaps. But he has observed it, day by day, through near half a century: he has seen his elders pass, by the hundreds, baffled and withered and yet, in some pathetic way, content enough: so that he knows in general terms what old age too is like.

Thus does it come about that to whosoever reaches forty-five the entire average course of human life has been displayed in somewhat the bewildering fashion of a moving picture of which the first and second halves are being shown simultaneously on the same screen. The spectator has got little enough out of it, God knows. Even so, he has the sad advantage of one who has not yet witnessed the inconsequent, astounding jumble. He at least has perceived it all with his own senses: he has perceived, with an immediacy which no report can parallel, what actually does befall the average man between the hours of birth and death: and it remains an affair of which his knowledge, howsoever blurred, and howsoever limited, comes to him at first hand. He is not dependent, as his juniors yet stay necessarily dependent, as even the superior thirties yet stay dependent, upon guesswork and the statements of others and those extremely misleading posters in the lobby. . . . Or let us vary the figure. Let us say that the traveler who has made a journey, it matters not how unperceptive his nature, does, after all, know more about that particular journey than is ever revealed to the most faithful and the most imaginative student of guidebooks.

CHAPTER FOUR

Which Records a Strange Truism

Which Records a Strange Truism

THUS, then, the average of human life has been shown in its entirety to every man of forty-five. The verdicts vary: but you may note, even so, that after forty-five the cynic and the pessimist turn unaccountably mellow. Life, it would seem, like a trip to the dentist, is not so very bad, after all, once you have put up with it. Life does not bid fair, to the tiring eyes of forty-five, ever to become a perfect business: and to preserve any especial altruism at forty-five is to present a happily rare case of arrested development. But the point is that when the performance has been witnessed, in its entirety, and with one's own senses, then the average of human life does tend to seem well enough just as it stands. The lying and the mismanagement do not promise ever to be rectified: but that appears hardly an elegiac matter, after all; for middle age, I repeat, has mastered that invaluable gesture which is known as a shrug.

Such is the discovery made by all men at forty-five or thereabouts: such, if you so prefer to phrase it, is the illusion to which middle age becomes a victim: such, in any case, is the eternal crux between middle age and youth. Youth is credulous in many matters, but upon one single issue youth stays as iron and granite: youth does not even believe that life serves well enough just as it stands. To believe that such is just possibly the case remains the attested hall-mark of middle life. . . . Thereafter optimism develops insidiously: and the most of us sink, cackling thinly, into an amiable senescence.

CHAPTER FIVE

Which Chronicles an Offset

CHAPTER FIVE

Which Chronicles an Offset

BUT it is with the younger generation in letters, rather than in life, that I am here the more distinctly concerned, now that time dissevers me from both. . . . And in literary fields there exists at least one rather striking offset to that particular bit of knowledge to which I have just now referred as being acquired by most men at forty-five. It is that any writer who thus comes to forty-five has purchased his knowledge without — at best — improving upon his chances of communicating that knowledge.

For, after forty-five or thereabouts, it is inevitable that a writer should cease to develop as a writer, just as he ceases to develop as a mammal. No one of his faculties, whatsoever else may happen to them, can improve after that all-arresting date. Some few — though not many authors, it more or less inexplicably appears, — begin to fail earlier. But the average writer has reached his peak at, to my finding, forty; and with favoring luck, with all that he has learned of technique to counterbalance a perhaps lessened exuberance in creative power, he may retain that peak for some years. Yet this retention profits him little. He has nothing new to give: and you may look henceforward to get from him no surprises.

Ultimately this does not matter: and, where the writer is at all remembered, posterity selects, in a rough and ready and very often wrong-headed fashion, that which posterity esteems to be the best of this writer's work, without any need to bother over the relative order of its composition. But during the remainder of the man's career as a practising author this individuality which permeates the work of every writer worth his salt does matter a great deal, to the debit side of his ledger.

CHAPTER SIX

Which Becomes Reasonable

 Experto crede

CHAPTER SIX

Which Becomes Reasonable

FOR we ask — not at all illogically — that a new book shall contain something new. We expect, in fine, some element of surprise: and after a writer's style is fairly formed, after his talents have each been competently developed, that is precisely the one element which he cannot supply. There is, from his point of view, no reason why he should supply it. He is still — so does he think, perhaps rightly, perhaps in merciful illusion, — still at his best, such as that best is. Yet, even be he right, each book that he publishes is a disappointment, howsoever loyally concealed, to his readers; and his most excellent work no longer produces the same effect upon his readers, because that excellence is familiar.

Every considerate person must respect, for example, the genius of Mr. Kipling and of Mr. Shaw, of Mr. Wells and Mr. Bennett: yet the publication of a new book by any one of them is not, nowadays, an event in which it is possible to take real interest. It is an event which at bottom we deplore. And so is it with every writer whose manner has been admirable long enough to become familiar. He publishes perforce a book which in every essential we have already read, time and again. We purchase, in loyalty to old delight: but we labor through the text with a sort of unadmitted impatience, by which those braver persons who write book reviews are irritated far more candidly.

Meanwhile the report gets about that the man is making money out of his writing: and in the corrupting miasma of that rumor no literary reputation, howsoever lusty, can long survive. It follows thus that by the time a tolerably successful artist in letters is really in full control of his powers, such as they are, he is definitely, for the rest of his lifetime, outmoded. In fact, he has become in some sort a pest.

There is loss here for the reader, though, I confess, I can see no possible way out. But for the artist there is no weighty loss, nor any valid ground upon which, as it were, to repine. Every artist in letters must become, ere he reaches sixty, more or less of a nuisance to the world of current reading-matter: but that, after all, is not an affair with which he himself is vitally concerned. For this sybarite spoils paper, as I have elsewhere tried to explain, for his own diversion: he knows that the artist, lucky above all men, and alone of human beings, is sometimes, if only for a season, praised, and even is paid sound money, for diverting himself: and he knows, too, that to the artist, when the applause lessens and the autograph hunters depart, there still remains the chance — granted to him alone of human beings, — to continue to divert himself in precisely that way which he most prefers.

But from the front ranks of contemporary writers, from the ranks of those who exercise an actually vital and yet growing influence, an author at about the time of his fiftieth birthday must withdraw perforce. These ranks are being filled — again, perforce, — by the younger men who have at least the one indispensable quality. They are new.

CHAPTER SEVEN

Which Deals with the Deplorable

CHAPTER SEVEN

Which Deals with the Deplorable

MEANWHILE, I have said, " The average writer has reached his peak at, to my finding, forty: and with favoring luck, with all that he has learned of technique to counterbalance a perhaps lessened exuberance in creative power, he may retain that peak for some years." The trouble is that he does not retain it indefinitely: the trouble is that in no great while the creative power is quite surely lessened; and the technique does but play futilely with the picked bones of defunct talents. The trouble is, in brief, that even for the most prodigally gifted of creative writers the way lies, by and by, downhill forever.

It has been the fate of but too many of our more captivating prosateurs to outlive their powers (which was a venial and often an unavoidable happening), and to outlive the desire to write, and yet, whether out of sheer habit or out of man's normal need for an income, to go on writing, — which was in all respects a calamity. . . . Here my theme becomes difficult. For to name here the living were uncivil. It is politely possible, though, to point in one embracing gesture to Scott and Dickens and Thackeray, — inasmuch as their merits nowadays have no least concern with the demerits of *Castle Dangerous* or of *Edwin Drood* or of *Philip,* — and to recall the arid inferiority of these dead giants' later labors, without any more of human pleasure than we unavoidably get from our betters' downfall.

It is possible, too, to let the last-named speak for the three of them. " All I can do now," said Thackeray, — at about the time of his fiftieth birthday, — " is to bring out my old puppets, and put new bits of ribbon on them. I have told my tale in the novel department. I only repeat old things in a pleasant way. I have nothing new to say. I get sick of my task when I am ill, and I think, ' Good Heavens! what is all this story about! ' "

It is a query which has been echoed by his readers, and by the readers of Dickens, and by the readers of Scott, and by the readers of many another aging novelist. . . . I pause here. I am tempted. But I reflect, rather wistfully, that I had resolved to name no living American author.

I now regret that resolve. I would much like here to speak frankly of my own generation in American letters.

CHAPTER EIGHT

Which Slightly Anticipates

CHAPTER EIGHT

Which Slightly Anticipates

YES, I would very much like here to speak frankly of my own generation in American letters. For it was, in so far as it stays at all memorable, the first generation which criticized the polity of the United States. It was the first generation which said flatly: All is not well with this civilization. And it was, pre-eminently, the generation which destroyed taboos, — not all taboos, of course, but a great many of those fetishes which the preceding generations had all left in unmolested honor.

To the other side, it is a generation of which the present-day survivors appear, to my finding, a bit ludicrously to go on fighting battles that were won long ago. It is a generation which nowadays evinces a quite distressing tendency to preserve at all costs the posture of Ajax defying the lightnings under an unclouded sky. It has thus become, already, a depressingly comic spectacle. It has done its work successfully: and that gratifying fact is the one fact which this generation of writers who prided themselves upon facing all facts, will not face to-day. Instead, it goes on working at its some-while-since-finished job, and it tilts at dead dragons, rather dodderingly, in the beginning palsy of superannuation.

So is it that, speaking always under the correction of time, I would say this is a generation destined quite quickly to be huddled away, by man's common-sense, into oblivion. For this generation has said, All is not well. To say that is permitted; to say that is indeed a conventional gambit in every known branch of writing. But this generation thereafter proffered no panacea: and that especial form of reticence is not long permissible.

To the contrary it is most plain here that, just as Manuel told Coth, the dream is better. It is man's nature to seek the dream; he requires an ever-present recipe for the millennium; and he vitally needs faith in some panacea or another which by and by will correct all ills. This generation has proffered no such recipe: and that queer omission has suggested, howsoever obliquely, that just possibly no panacea may exist anywhere. This is a truth which man's intelligence can confront for no long while. He very much prefers that equivalent of hashish which I have seen described, in the better thought of and more tedious periodicals, as constructive criticism. Most properly, therefore, have those junior writers who were not ever harried by taboos, or by the draft laws, begun to suggest a tasteful variety of panaceas: and all persons blessed with common-sense, will eventually select, if but at random, some one or another of these recipes, wherein to invest faith, and wherefrom to extract comfort.

Meanwhile all intelligent persons will, moreover, put out of mind, as soon as may be possible, that unique and bothersome generation of writers who suggested no panacea whatever. . . . And meanwhile, too, as I have remarked a bit earlier, I intend in this place to say not anything about this generation.

Even so, you will see, I trust, my point. In

rough figures, all the available evidence tends to show that after fifty every creative writer labors in an ever-thickening shadow of decadence. There may be exceptions; I believe that, if they indeed exist, they are few: and, in any case, one does not build upon exceptions.

Which Keeps a Long Standing Engagement

CHAPTER NINE

Which Keeps a Long Standing Engagement

I DETERMINED, therefore, now some ten years ago, to finish the Biography before I had passed fifty, if it were granted me to live that long; and afterward to add no line to, and to change in nothing, the Biography. The Biography of the life of Manuel seems now, to my partial gaze, a completed performance.

With the lateliest added of my comedies — I allude to *Something About Eve,* the last of my books to have any general circulation, — the reviewers have dealt in a sufficing vein of pleasantness; moreover, the book has evoked dispraise from all the desirable quarters; and for a respectable, but not incriminating, number of weeks did the Comedy of Fig-leaves also figure in the lists of " best sellers."

The autograph hunters, Heaven and the post-man be my witnesses, have not yet departed. I find that, day in, day out, I mail to "collectors" rather more of my book plates than I paste in my books. I am still favored with invitations to ad-dress, if but gratis, the local woman's club in some town of which I had not previously heard. I am honored now and then with the suggestion that I present my collected works, with each volume suitably inscribed and signed, to one or another public library. School children write me every day or so, requesting that I prepare for them a sketch of my life, illustrated with at least two photo-graphs, of my home and person, and that I add thereto a full critical account of the books which I have written and my general æsthetic theories. They desire in particular to know the names of my books.

Meanwhile, young men continue to solicit my tuition in black magic and my opinion of journal-ism as a profession. Only yesterday I received a letter from a thitherto-unknown-to-me young lady of the Middle West who is conducting "an ex-perimental study of love" and had thought of me as a possible collaborator. Wives write to me about their husbands, quite explicitly. Beginning authors yet favor me with the manuscripts of novels which they desire me to rewrite and get published for them. Entire strangers still ring my doorbell upon the plea that they are in town only for the day and would like to spend that day with me. . . . I may consider myself, in fine, for all that my books have not ever sold in such quantities as a publisher might reasonably prefer, to be honored with a fair allotment of the annoyances of notoriety, now that I come to be fifty.

Let none mistake me here. I have already enumerated those causes which must lead every considerate person to believe that bleak oblivion and general disregard await me, beyond any rational doubt, in common with all the writers of my generation. My point is merely that at this especial season I find myself to be, as yet, appreciably far from either reward. My point is that this especial season would therefore seem the happiest and the most fit time to wind up the long enterprise of the Biography, while everyone concerned stays, as yet, in a fairly genial humor. My point, in brief, is that the date which I had set for the winding up of the Biography's affairs turns out to be, after all, a rather well chosen date, now that I come to finish, in *The Way of Ecben,* the last of all the many stories about the many inheritors of Dom Manuel's life.

CHAPTER TEN

Which, at Long Last, Says All

Which, at Long Last, Says All

I NEVERTHELESS regret that there may henceforward come from my typewriter no more stories about Ettarre, who has been always, I confess, the most dear to me of Dom Manuel's daughters. My comfort is that there will always be new stories about Ettarre, under one or another name, by the writers who shall come after my decaying generation. For all the young men everywhere that were poets have had their glimpse of her loveliness, and they have heard a cadence or two of that troubling music which accompanies the passing of Ettarre; and they have made, and they will make forever, their stories about the witch-woman, so long as youth endures among mankind and April punctually returns into the world which men inhabit.

But we who are not young any longer, and who, despite our memories, yet must behold Ettarre and all things else with the eyes which time has given us, and who (despite how many glowing memories) must yet find in her music, nowadays, no more than did old Alfgar, — we may not dare to depend upon mere memories, howsoever splendid and dear, to piece out for us any more tales as to Ettarre the witch-woman. For memories alone remain. We may well dare, as Alfgar dared, to preserve our faith in that which is beyond and above us: but we would wiseliest keep faith, even so, in silence as to that which our lean human senses now deny. For memories alone remain. We that have reached our middle life may not any longer behold Ettarre with that clearness which is granted to our juniors: and this is an unpleasant fact, this is indeed in some sort an ever restive taunt, which must, to-day and for all time, obscurely discontent the living of every poet who has entered into his prosaic and over quiet fifties, and who has discovered, quietly, that of the lad who followed after Ettarre now memories alone remain.

Even so, you have heard what all these maimed and discontented poets yet cry to the witch-